The Magic Brush

...and other stories

Enid Blyton®

The Magic Brush

...and other stories

Bounty Books

Published in 2014 by Bounty Books,
a division of Octopus Publishing Group Ltd,
Carmelite House
50 Victoria Embankment
London EC4Y 0DZ
www.octopusbooks.co.uk

An Hachette UK Company
www.hachette.co.uk

Illustrated by Sara Voller.

ISBN: 978-0-75372-674-7

A CIP catalogue record for this book is available from the British Library.

Printed and bound by CPI Group (UK) Ltd, Croydon, CR0 4YY

3 5 7 9 10 8 6 4

CONTENTS

1

The Magic Brush

Once upon a time Dame Lazybones went to do a little spring-cleaning at Wizard Twinkle's castle. She was just like her name, and never did a thing unless she had to.

Now, when she got to the castle Wizard Twinkle was just going out. 'Good morning, Dame,' he said. 'Please scrub all the floors to-day - and do them well!'

He slammed the great door, and Dame Lazybones sighed and groaned. How dreadful to have to do so much work all at once! Then she spied something that made her chuckle with delight. The wizard had left out his magic book of spells. The old dame ran to it and turned up 'Scrubbing brush.' She soon found what she wanted.

'To make a brush scrub by magic,' she read, 'take an ordinary brush, lay it down on its back, trip round it three times, cry, "Romany-ree" as you go, and then kick the brush in the air, saying "Scrub away, brush!"'

In great delight the old woman took the scrubbing-brush, laid it down on its back, and tripped round it three times,

crying loudly 'Romany-ree!' Then up into the air she kicked the brush, shouting 'Scrub away, brush!'

The brush fell to the ground and then, to Dame Lazybones' great delight, it began to scrub the floor all by itself. You should have seen it! There was a large pail of soapy water just nearby, and the brush kept going to this and dipping itself in, and then scrubbing

the floor with a fine, shishoo-shishoo-shishoo noise.

'Ah,' said Dame Lazybones, sitting herself down in the wizard's own armchair with a pleased smile. 'This is the best way to work - sitting down and watching something else!'

Well, it wasn't long before the old dame was fast asleep, and she snored gently whilst the scrubbing-brush went on working busily. It finished the floor of that room and went to the next. Then it went upstairs and did the bedroom floors. They were all of stone, and very dirty indeed, so the brush really did work hard.

At last all the floors were finished. The brush sat up on its end and looked round for something else to scrub. Ah yes! It would scrub the walls.

So it began. But it didn't like the pictures that hung here and there so it sent those down with a crash to the floor. That woke up Dame Lazybones, and she looked at the brush in horror.

'Stop! Stop!' she shouted. 'Whatever are you doing? Are you mad, brush?'

But the brush didn't stop. It began scrubbing the top of the stove and sent five saucepans, three kettles and a frying-pan flying off with great clangs and bangs. Dame Lazybones rushed to the magic book and looked up the spell again - but to her great dismay there was nothing there about how to stop a magic brush from working. She didn't know what in the world to do. She rushed at the brush just as it was going into the larder, and tried to snatch it.

Crack! It gave her such a rap on the knuckles that she cried out with pain. She tried to get hold of it again, and once more it tapped her smartly on the hand. Then it popped into the kitchen cupboard and began to scrub the shelves, sending everything flying out into the kitchen.

'Oof!' said Dame Lazybones as a milk pudding landed on her shoulder. 'Ow!' she cried as a jelly slipped down her neck. Crash! Smash! Down went

dishes of jam-tarts, tins of cakes, joints of meat on the floor - and dear me, a large bottle of milk crashed down near the surprised kitchen cat, who at once began to lick it up with joy.

'Stop! Stop!' cried Dame Lazybones, in horror, to the excited brush. But nothing would make it stop! It went next to the windows and began to scrub those, and down came all the curtains on the floor.

And just at that moment the door opened and in came Wizard Twinkle! Oh my, how Dame Lazybones shivered and shook.

'Oh, stop the brush, stop it!' she cried. But the wizard shook his head. 'It has one more job to do!' he said - and as he spoke, the brush flew over to poor Dame Lazybones and began to scrub her too! Oh, what a state she was in! How she ran, how she fought that brush - but it wasn't a bit of good, it gave her a good drubbing, rubbing and scrubbing!

Then the wizard clapped his hands and said, 'Romany-ree, come to me!' The brush hopped over to him, stood by his foot and did nothing more.

'See what your laziness has done!' said the wizard, looking all round with a frown at the dreadful mess everywhere. 'You will now clean up this place from top to bottom, Dame Lazybones - and never let me hear of your being LAZY again!'

'Oh, no sir, no sir!' wept Dame Lazybones as she hurried to pick up all the things lying on the floor. 'Oh, I'll never be lazy again! Oh, that dreadful brush! Oh, deary, deary me!'

And you'll be glad to know that the old dame never *was* lazy again; she couldn't forget that magic brush!

2

The Horrid Little Boy

Benny was a horrid little boy. He was cross, spiteful, and snappy, and his mother often scolded him for being so unkind to his brothers and sisters.

'You always behave well when your daddy is at home,' said his mother. 'But as soon as he is out of the house you behave more like an animal than a little boy - growling and snapping and snarling at your brothers and sisters like a bad-tempered little dog!'

Now one day Benny behaved badly when his father was at home - which was a great mistake, because his father was strict and wouldn't stand any nonsense at all!

It happened at dinner-time. All the children were sitting round the table, eating, and their father and mother were one at each end. Benny was grumbling because he hadn't got as

much fruit salad as the others - and, when he thought no one was looking he scooped a big piece of pear from his brother's plate on to his own!

His brother saw him and tried to get it back. Benny made a noise like a growl, and slapped his brother in the face. Over went the plate of fruit salad, and his father jumped up in a rage.

'Benny! You behave worse than the dog under the table! If you can't behave like a little boy, you can join the dog. Go on the mat!'

Well! Think of that! Benny didn't know what to do! But he knew he had to obey, so up he got and went over to the mat.

'Lie down on the mat,' said his father in a stern voice, just as if he were speaking to Twister, the dog.

Benny lay down. He felt very silly, especially as all the other children began to laugh at him.

He had to stay there till the meal was finished. Then he began to cry.

'I'm still hungry,' he said to his

mother. His father went to the kitchen and fetched a bone from the stock-pot.

'Here you are,' he said. 'Here's a bone for you. Keep it on the mat.'

Oh dear, oh dear! So Benny was to be

fed like a dog too! He looked at the bone, but he couldn't touch it! Nasty, horrid, hard bone!

'I'm thirsty!' he whined.

His father put down a bowl of water for him.

'Now, any more whining from you, Benny, and I shall fetch the whip!' he said, just as if Benny was Twister.

That afternoon the children's father said he would take them to the park to have a good time on the swings there. Benny jumped up from the mat in delight. It was fun to have a swing in the park. His father saw him and shouted to him:

'Down, Benny, down! Lie down, do you hear!'

'I don't want to be treated like a dog,' sulked Benny.

'If you behave like one you must expect to be treated like one!' said his father. 'Lie down!'

So Benny had to lie down on the mat

till the children were ready. Then off they all started, running down the lane eagerly - but Benny was made to walk just at his father's heels with Twister.

'Walk to heel, Benny, walk to heel, Twister,' ordered his father. So, whilst the others were laughing and running, Benny had to walk to heel like Twister. How the others laughed at him, and cried, 'Good dog, Benny, good dog!'

When they got to the park the children raced to the swings - but

Benny was made to lie down with Twister on the grass by his father's feet, whilst his father read the paper. After a while Twister licked his master's hand and whined gently.

'Do you want a run, old chap?' said his master. 'Well, off you go, then, once round the park and back. Go with him, Benny - straight round and back. Do you hear me?'

Benny hated running just round the park and back when he wanted to go and play, but he did as he was told. When he got back, it was time to go home. He had to walk to heel again with Twister.

It was tea-time when they got home - and what a delicious smell of new-made chocolate cake greeted the hungry children! Benny sniffed in delight, and ran to the kitchen.

'Come here, Benny, come here!' roared his father to Benny. 'Lie down, I tell you!'

Benny had to go back to the mat and lie down with Twister – and oh, what a very dreadful disappointment, no one took any notice of him at tea-time, and his mother didn't even offer him a piece of the chocolate cake.

'I'm hungry!' wept poor Benny.

'Dogs don't have tea,' said his father. 'You must wait till six, when Twister has his dry biscuits.'

After tea his father went out into the yard, and Benny heard him hammering away at something. The other children peeped out of the window, and one of

them cried out, 'Oh, Daddy is making a kennel for Benny! He will have to sleep out in the yard to-night with Twister! Oh, he will really be a little dog then!'

But that was too much for Benny. He got up from the mat and ran crying to his mother in the kitchen.

'Mother! Mother! I don't want to be a dog any more! I want to be a little boy. I'm sorry I was so horrid! I'll never be so unkind again! I can't bear being all alone. It's horrid to be a dog if you aren't really!'

His mother put her arms round him.

'Well, Benny,' she said, 'you have been very unkind and spiteful lately – even Twister would not behave so badly. It is no use expecting people to treat you nicely if you don't behave nicely. Go and tell your father what you mean to do.'

So Benny ran out to his father and told him that he was never going to behave like a spiteful little snappy dog again. He was going to be a nice little boy. His father believed him, and said,

'Well, Benny, I'll take your word for it. Go indoors, and see if Mother has saved you a piece of that chocolate cake after all.'

She had - and Benny did enjoy it. He ate it from a plate, sitting at the table, not on the mat - and didn't it feel nice to be a little boy again?

Well, that was last week - and since then Benny has been the nicest boy you can imagine, kind, thoughtful, and polite. I hope it will last - it would be so dreadful if he had to live on the mat again, wouldn't it! Twister *would* be astonished!

3

The Disappearing Hats

Once upon a time, in the Village of Get-About, there was a hat-shop. Two gnomes owned it, Sniffle and Snuffle. They made excellent top-hats in all colours - blue, pink, yellow, and green, for the folk of Get-About went to a great many meetings and parties, and wore top-hats very often.

And then a strange thing happened. The top-hats belonging to the people of Get-About began to disappear in a very peculiar way!

Burly-One, the gnome, had just bought a magnificent green one with a yellow band round it. He wore it to a meeting in the next village and felt very smart indeed. He came home and hung it up as usual in the hall. The next day it wasn't there!

Then another hat disappeared. This time it was Curly-top's hat. He was a pixie and had a very choice top-hat – pink with a blue band, and he had stuck a little feather in at the side. He had put his in a box on a shelf in his bedroom – but bless us all, when he looked in the box the next day, the hat was gone! The only thing in the box was the little feather.

When Curly-top and Burly-One met and began to tell one another about

their vanished hats, two others came up and said theirs had gone too!

'I put mine on the kitchen-table,' said Bong, the brownie. 'And this morning it wasn't there.'

'And I put mine on the knob at the end of my bed,' said Chortle, the elf. 'And I know it was there when I went to sleep, because my wife said to me, 'Chortle, you've put your hat on the knob again instead of in its box.' So I know it was there – and this morning it was gone!'

'And there's the party to-day at Lord High-and-Mighty's,' groaned Burly-One. 'What are we to do? We *must* go in top-hats!'

'We'd better go to Sniffle and Snuffle and see if they have any hats to fit us,' said Curly-top. 'I don't expect they will have.'

They went to the gnomes' shop and explained to them about their vanished hats. Sniffle and Snuffle listened and looked very surprised indeed.

'Now the thing is, Sniffle and Snuffle,'

said Bong, 'we've got this party this afternoon. Can you possibly let us have top-hats in time?'

'I suppose you'd like them just the same as your others?' said Sniffle.

'Yes,' said everyone.

'Well, we'll try to manage them in time,' said Sniffle. 'But we are afraid we will have to charge you more than usual, as we shall have to work so hard.'

'Oh dear!' groaned Chortle. 'Well, I suppose it can't be helped.'

Exactly ten minutes before Curly-top, Burly-One, Chortle, and Bong were ready to set off to their party, their hats arrived from Sniffle and Snuffle. They each put them on in delight. Really, they might have been the same hats they had lost! They fitted perfectly.

Now that night three other hats disappeared belonging to Fee, Fi and Fo, three brother goblins. They were terribly upset because they had to go to a most important meeting that day - and how could they be seen out without their fine top-hats?

'I put mine in my bedroom on the top of the wardrobe,' said Fee.

'And I hung mine on the chair,' said Fi.

'I don't know where I put mine, but it was *some*where!' groaned Fo.

'We'd better go to Sniffle and Snuffle and see if they can let us have hats in time,' said Fee. So off they went - and the two gnomes promised to work hard and send three hats in good time.

'But we shall have to charge you more money,' said Sniffle.

Now as more and more top-hats disappeared the people of Get-About Village became very angry. They lay in wait for the robbers whom they thought must come to steal their hats - but never a robber did they see! It was all most peculiar.

The only people who didn't mind about the disappearing hats were Sniffle and Snuffle, who did a roaring trade, and charged every one more than usual because they were so busy and had to work so hard.

At last Fee, Fi and Fo, whose hats had disappeared for the second time, went to visit the wise woman, Dame Thinkitout. She listened to their tale and then nodded her head. 'So you want to find the thieves?' she said. 'Well, tie a long, long string to your hats, goblins, and then, when they

disappear, follow the string and you'll find the thieves at the end of it!'

'What a good idea!' said Fee, Fi and Fo. They went home and each of them carefully tied a very very long string to his hat. One end was round the hat, and the other was tied tightly to the bed knob.

Nothing happened that night – but the next night the goblins were awakened by a strange whistling sound. They lighted a candle. Their hats were gone!

'Quick!' said Fee, tumbling out of bed. 'We must follow the strings!'

They found that the strings went out of the window - down the garden, across the road, over the long meadow, down the hill - and into - where do you think? Why, into Sniffle and Snuffle's shop! Yes, really!

The goblins peeped into the shop through a crack in the curtain. They saw Sniffle and Snuffle there. Sniffle was standing in the middle of the room, chanting a magic rhyme, and Snuffle was standing with his arms out to catch the hats that came in at the window!

'Oh! the wicked robbers!' said Fee, Fi and Fo angrily. 'They make our top-hats - and put a disappearing spell in them so that they can get them back - and then sell them to us again for more money than before!'

The goblins all climbed in at the

window and began to shout at the surprised gnomes.

'Robbers! Thieves! Wait till the people of Get-About hear what we've found out! Yes – just wait till to-morrow morning!'

'Mercy, mercy!' begged the two gnomes pale with fright.

'Certainly not!' said Fee, and pinched Sniffle's long nose. He had wanted to do that for a long time. 'Give us our hats!'

The goblins took their hats, put them on, and stalked out of the shop. 'Aha! You wait till to-morrow!' said Fo.

You can guess how angry the folk of Get-About were when they heard all that Fee, Fi and Fo had to tell them. They marched to the gnomes' shop next morning – but it was closed! A notice hung outside. 'GONE AWAY. YOU CAN ALL EAT YOUR HATS!'

'What cheek!' snorted Chortle, in a rage.

'Well, we can at any rate use the hats they've had to leave behind!' said

SPELLS
SPELLS

Bong. There were heaps of top-hats in the shop. The folk of Get-About tried them on. There were enough for everyone to have two or three.

'I'm glad I pulled Sniffle's long nose last night,' said Fee. 'I wish I had pulled Snuffle's too!'

Nobody knows what became of the two bad gnomes - and a very good thing too!

4

Santa Claus Gets a Shock

It was Christmas Eve. Betty and Fred were in bed, talking quietly. Mother had tucked them up and said good night a long time ago.

'We shall hear quite well if Santa Claus lands on our roof,' said Betty, 'because our house is a bungalow, and the roof is very low. Shall we listen for him, Fred? It's getting near midnight.'

'Yes, let's,' said Fred. 'I'd love to hear him come. We shall hear the reindeer hooves on the roof quite easily!'

So they lay and listened - and do you know, in a few minutes they heard the sound of sleigh-bells ringing in the distance!

Both children sat up in bed in excitement. 'Do you hear that, Betty?'

said Fred. 'It's Santa Claus! Now we'll hear the reindeer on the roof!'

But they didn't! The bells came nearer and nearer, and then stopped except for a tinkle now and then.

'That's funny,' said Fred. 'Santa Claus didn't land on the roof to come down our chimney.'

'Well, where did he land then?' said Betty. 'He must have landed somewhere! I hope he didn't try to land on the garden shed or the greenhouse!'

'We should have heard the tinkle of breaking glass if he'd tried to land on

the greenhouse roof,' said Fred with a giggle.

Just then they did hear the sound of something breaking - but it didn't sound like glass. They wondered whatever it could be. They sat and listened. Then they heard the sound of bells again, rather soft - and suddenly there came the noise of a very soft thudding at the window.

'Goodness! Do you suppose it's Santa Claus trying to come in at the window?' said Betty, excited. 'You open it, Fred - hurry!'

The soft thudding came again - knock-knock-knock! Fred slipped out of bed and ran to the window. He drew back the curtain and opened the window.

And whatever do you suppose was

poked in at the open window? Guess! It was the long soft nose of a brown reindeer! Yes, in came the nose, and nuzzled up to Fred.

Then beside the first long nose came another - and another and another! Four large-eyed reindeer looked in at that window!

'It was their noses we heard knocking on the window-pane!' cried Betty. 'What do they want? Is Santa Claus there?'

'No,' said Fred, puzzled, peering out of the window. One of the reindeer plucked hold of the little boy's pyjama sleeve and began to pull him gently.

'Let go!' said Fred in surprise. 'You'll pull me out of the window.'

'That's what he wants to do, Fred,' said Betty, watching. 'Look - here's your dressing-gown and your shoes. Put them on, and I'll put mine on too. I think the reindeer have come to fetch us for something.'

As soon as the four reindeer saw the children putting on their clothes, they stopped pulling at Fred's sleeve. They stood patiently at the window, waiting, their bells tinkling very softly as they moved now and again.

The children climbed out of the window on to the grass outside. They had both got their torches, and they flashed them on to see where Santa Claus was.

And what do *you* think had happened to poor old Santa Claus? He had gone across the garden with his big sack of toys, and had walked right over the thinly-frozen pond, without knowing it was there - and the ice had broken, and into the pond had tumbled Santa Claus, toys and all! The reindeer had seen him and come to Fred and Betty for help.

The pond was large and deep. As soon as Fred saw what had happened, he ran to the garden shed. He got a rope from there and threw it to Santa Claus. Then very carefully he and

Betty dragged out the poor, wet old man!

'Oh, Santa Claus! What a shame that you should have fallen into our pond!' said Betty. 'You must be so cold and wet! Why didn't you land on our roof?'

'Well, your house is a small bungalow and I never land on bungalow roofs,' said Santa Claus. 'I'm too easily seen from the road if I do – so I usually land in the garden then. Is there anywhere that I can dry myself?'

'We've a fire in the kitchen,' said Fred. 'Everyone is in bed and asleep, so come along and get dry. Aren't your reindeer clever to come and fetch us to help you, Santa!'

The children took Santa Claus into their bedroom and then led the way quietly to the kitchen. There was a nice fire there. Tibs, the cat, was sitting by it. She seemed delighted to see Santa Claus.

'Hello! There's the cat I brought you for a present last year when she was a kitten!' said Santa. 'I remember that she wouldn't stay in your stocking, Betty! Hello, Puss! You've grown into a nice cat!'

Betty made up the fire, feeling really excited. The little girl got a saucepan and poured some milk in it to put on the stove to heat for poor, cold Santa Claus. He took off his wet coat and boots, and did his best to squeeze the water out of his trousers.

'Ah! I shall soon be dry in front of this nice hot fire,' he said. 'Well, it's kind of you children to rescue me! My goodness! I didn't want to spend the night in your pond, I can tell you.'

'Tell us a story, Santa Claus,' begged Betty. So the jolly old chap began to tell the two children how all the toys were made in his enormous castle.

'And, you know, even when the toys are made, they still are not ready to go with me,' said Santa. 'The teddy bears have to be taught to growl - and you wouldn't believe how stupid some of them are! Do you know, I had a bear last year who would keep thinking he was a duck - and every time I pressed his tummy he said, 'Quack, quack!''

The children laughed. 'I do wish you'd given him to *us*,' said Fred. 'He would have made us laugh. Tell us some more, Santa Claus.'

'Well, another time I had a doll that we had to teach to open and shut her eyes,' said Santa, turning himself round so that the fire might dry his back. 'And do you know, she *would* wrinkle her nose and screw up her mouth every time she opened and shut her eyes. So we couldn't give her to anybody either! Fancy having a doll that did that!'

'I think she sounds lovely,' said Betty, imagining a doll that wrinkled her little nose and screwed up her rosebud mouth.

'And another time I had a . . .' began Santa Claus - and then he suddenly stopped and listened. There was a noise at the kitchen door. He went and opened the door - and in walked the four reindeer, dragging the sleigh behind them!

'Oh no! Oh no!' said Santa, trying to push them out. 'You can wait for me outside. How dare you walk in here as if it was your stable!'

The children laughed loudly. It was so funny to see Santa pushing the reindeer on the noses, making them go out backwards, their bells jingling. But they had forgotten that their father and mother were asleep in their bedroom not far off!

And suddenly they heard the sound of their mother's light being switched on. 'That's mother waking up!' said Fred, in a fright. 'Quick, drink up your milk Santa! Mother may see you. We'll have to pop back to bed!'

Santa drank up the hot milk, snatched up his clothes and his sack, and disappeared into the garden. The children ran to go to their bedroom – but

their mother came into the kitchen before they could escape.

'Betty! Fred! How very naughty of you! And you have been heating milk for yourselves too! I suppose you thought you would see Santa Claus if you waited up so late. Really, it's very naughty of you. Anyway, there isn't such a person as Santa Claus!'

'Oh, Mother, there is! He's just been here,' said Fred. 'We heated the milk for *him*. He fell into our pond and got so wet.'

'Don't tell naughty stories,' said Mother, really cross with them.

'Well, Mother, can't you hear the sleigh-bells?' said Betty. She heard them quite clearly as Santa Claus galloped off. 'Oh, Mother, I wish you hadn't come in quite so soon - because now Santa Claus has galloped away without leaving us any presents!'

Mother hustled them into bed and tucked them up again. The children were sad. They were very tired too, and in a few moments they were asleep.

And do you know, in the morning they found two very peculiar toys sitting on the end of their beds! One was a teddy bear that said 'Quack, quack!' instead of growling, and the other was a doll who wrinkled her nose and screwed up her mouth whenever she shut and opened her eyes!

'So it *couldn't* have been a dream!' said Betty, hugging her doll. 'Oh, Fred – aren't we lucky?'

I think they *were* lucky, don't you?

5

Ragged Old Monkey

It was Geoffrey's birthday, and he had such a lovely lot of presents! You should have seen them! There was a shining new engine with four carriages, a large white teddy bear with an enormous growl, a clockwork soldier that marched across the floor when he was wound up, and a real live puppy! Wasn't he lucky?

Geoffrey was very pleased with his presents. 'I shall have a lovely time playing with them to-day,' he said to his mother.

He took them all to the nursery. They looked round to see what sort of a home they had come into. It looked very nice. The nursery was big and sunny, and there was a fine toy cupboard in it.

'Plenty of room for us there,' said the teddy bear, with a low growl.

Then no more was said by the toys until Geoffrey stopped playing with them and went off to have his dinner. Then the new toys and the puppy were left on the nursery floor together.

They began to talk.

'Did you ever see quite such an enormous bear as I am?' said the teddy, giving such a deep growl that the puppy jumped up in alarm, and looked about to see if there was another dog in the room! 'I was the biggest bear in the toy shop and the most expensive.

I think Geoffrey is very lucky to have me. I am sure he will take me to sleep with him in his bed at night.'

'I was expensive too,' said the clockwork soldier. 'Did you see how well I marched across the floor this morning? I am sure Geoffrey will think I am the cleverest toy he has!'

'Well, he will play with *me* the most!' said the shining engine with its four trucks. 'All boys like engines and railways better than anything. You will see that I will be his favourite!'

'Ah, but wait till I grow up a bit!' said the puppy, with a wuff. 'I shall go with him on all his walks, and he will be fonder of me than of any of you. I'm alive, you see, and you are not!'

'You don't know what you are talking about,' said the bear with a cross growl. 'I cost fifty pounds, and Geoffrey will be sure to think I am his very best playmate.'

Suddenly another voice spoke, and the bear, the soldier, the train, and the puppy looked round in surprise. Some one had come out of the big toy cupboard.

'Good day to you,' said a husky voice. 'Welcome to our nursery!'

A ragged old toy monkey had come out of the cupboard door. He had only one eye and one ear, his tail was so thin that it looked like a bit of string, and he was patched and darned all over his body.

'Whatever are *you?*' said the bear, in disgust. 'What a dirty, ragged creature you are!'

'Keep away from *me!*' said the soldier, wrinkling up his wooden nose. 'I am sure you smell horrid.'

'What is that creature doing in this nice nursery?' said the engine, in a scornful voice.

'Wuff!' said the puppy, and ran at the monkey. 'You ragged old thing! Go away! You ought to be thrown out! How *could* Geoffrey have you here with us?'

'Geoffrey is fond of me,' said the

monkey, in a gentle voice. 'Don't be silly, new toys and puppy. I have only come out to bid you welcome - do not be rude to me.'

'Who could help being rude to a dirty old thing like you!' cried the bear.

The monkey said no more, but went back into the cupboard. The toys and the puppy talked to one another loudly, and made rude remarks about the ragged old monkey.

That afternoon Geoffrey was to have a birthday party. He was dressed in his best suit and had his hair brushed till it shone. Just at four o'clock, when his friends were expected, he came rushing into the nursery.

'Who's coming to my party?' he shouted, in excitement. 'Bear, you're too big! Puppy, you're too noisy! Engine, you wouldn't do! Soldier, you're amusing, but I don't want to keep winding you up. I know – where's ragged old monkey? Monkey, where are you?

Come on! You shall go to the party! You've been to all my parties so far, and you shan't miss this one!'

He opened the cupboard door and dragged out the monkey. Then down the stairs he rushed, just as the first guest came knocking at the door.

'Well!' said the bear, in disgust. 'Think of that! Choosing that awful, dirty, ragged monkey instead of any of *us*. What a strange boy!'

'I should have amused the children very much,' said the clockwork soldier in a hurt voice.

'So should I,' said the puppy crossly. 'I should have nibbled every one's shoes!'

'And I would have rushed round the room at top speed,' said the engine.

'What can that monkey do? Nothing at all! He just looks ragged and smells dirty! Stupid, one-eyed, one-eared thing!'

The party went on, and was a great success. When it was over Geoffrey brought monkey upstairs and put him into the cupboard. Then he went to his bedroom to undress.

The monkey began to tell about the party, and all the toys in the cupboard listened eagerly. But the three new toys and the puppy were very rude.

'Who wants to hear about a silly old party?' they shouted. 'Be quiet, ragged monkey! You talk too much! Who are you, we should like to know, to talk and talk and talk when there are far better people in the room than *you!*'

'Oh, hush!' cried the toys in the cupboard. 'You must not talk like that to monkey.'

'We shall talk as we like!' said the bear, 'and what is more, I expect Geoffrey will take me to bed with him to-night, and I shall whisper into his ear that he must get rid of that ragged old monkey. I will *not* live in the same nursery with him!'

'I'll drag him out of the cupboard and bite his other ear off!' said the puppy. He went to the cupboard and dragged out the frightened monkey - but just as he was going to bite him, Geoffrey came into the room in his pyjamas.

'Good night toys,' he began - and then he saw what the puppy was doing. At once he ran to rescue the monkey, and he gave the puppy such a slap that he yelped in fright.

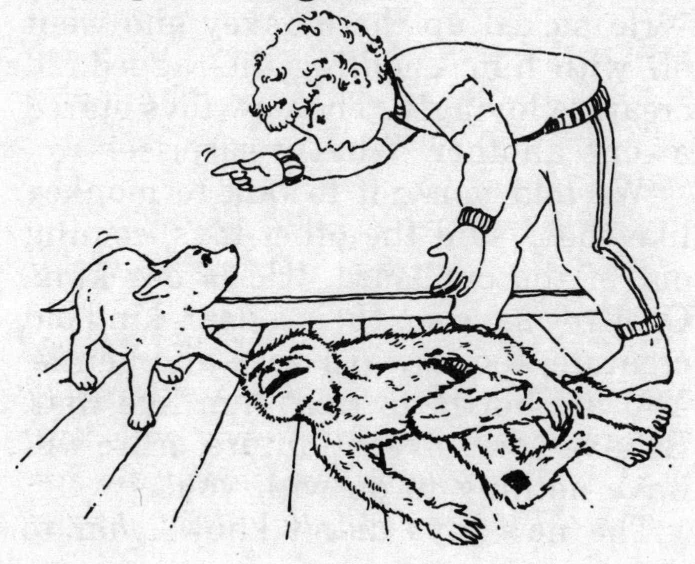

'How dare you! how dare you!' cried Geoffrey. 'I won't have my darling old monkey treated like that! You'll go and live in the kitchen if you treat him so roughly. I've just come to fetch him because he always goes to bed with me at night. I love him best of all my toys. He is the very oldest and nicest one. I know he is dirty and ragged, but that doesn't matter - I love him very much, and I always will. He is king of all the toys, so just remember that puppy and teddy bear, soldier and engine!'

He picked up the monkey and went off with him, cuddling the ragged old creature lovingly. The new toys stared at one another. What a surprise!

'We told you not to talk to monkey like that,' said the other toys, coming out of the cupboard. 'He is our king. Geoffrey says so. He is a dear, kind old creature, too, always wise and gentle. You are horrid to treat him like that. Behave yourselves in future, or we will have nothing to do with you!'

The new toys didn't know *what* to

say! They were horrified to find they had been so rude to the king of the toys. Whatever would happen to them?

Well, nothing happened, of course, for the monkey was too kind to punish them as they deserved. They soon grew to love him, and whenever his birthday comes round they cheer loudly with all the rest.

'Hip, hip, hurray for ragged old monkey!'

6

A Bit of Blue Sky

Harry and Joan badly wanted to go out in the garden to play, because Harry had a Red Indian hat of bright feathers, and he and Joan wanted to take turns at wearing it. It would be such fun to play Red Indians!

They went to the nursery window and looked out. The sky was full of clouds - big grey clouds that slid along in the wind.

Old Nannie Wimple was sitting in the nursery, knitting. She had been Daddy's Nannie when he was little, and she was very old. She had come to look after the children whilst Mummy was away, and dear me, the stories she knew, and the things she could tell Harry and Joan! It was marvellous!

A Bit of Blue Sky

'Nannie Wimple, do you think we shall be able to go out after dinner?' asked Harry. 'Or is it going to rain?'

Nannie didn't look up from her knitting. Her needles went click-clack all the time. 'Is there enough blue sky to make a sailor a pair of trousers?' she said.

Harry and Joan stared at Nannie Wimple in surprise. What a funny thing to say!

'Why do you say that, Nannie?' asked Joan.

'Well, haven't you heard the saying that the day will be fine if you can see enough blue in the sky to make a sailor a pair of trousers?' asked Nannie Wimple.

'I think I did hear Mummy say that one day,' said Harry. 'Will it really be fine if we see enough blue sky to do that, Nannie?'

'It's quite likely to be,' said Nannie.

The two children looked up into the sky. At first they could see nothing but clouds. Then two clouds came a little

apart, and the blue sky shone through, so bright that it was like a patch of forget-me-nots.

'Look!' said Joan. 'There's some blue! But, Nannie, I don't know if it's big enough to make a sailor a pair of trousers! I really don't know how much would be needed!'

'Dear, dear, these children!' said Nannie, sticking her two needles into the knitting wool and getting up to come to the window. 'I suppose I'll have to find out for you.'

'But, Nannie, however can you find out?' asked Harry in surprise.

'My great-grandmother taught me a little magic,' said Nannie. The two children suddenly felt excited. Magic! Oooh! Whatever was Nannie going to do?

'I'll get that bit of blue sky down for you, and we'll measure it up and see if there's enough for a sailor,' said Nannie. The children stared at her in surprise.

'How can you do that?' said Joan.

Nannie took a pair of big scissors, put her arm out as far as she could, and pretended to cut the shape of the blue bit of sky. All the time she muttered some very queer-sounding words. The children knew they were magic words, and they listened in delight.

Nannie stopped muttering. She slipped her scissors into her apron pocket and pointed to the sky.

'Watch!' she said. 'That bit of blue will fall down.'

And do you know, it did! It shook itself away from the sky and began to fall to earth, getting bigger and bigger as it came! It was most extraordinary to see it tumbling down like a big blue cloth, the colour of forget-me-nots.

It fell down and down, flapping in the wind. It came into the garden! It flapped on the grass, and the children squealed for joy.

'Look! It's on the lawn! Let's go and get it!'

They rushed out to get it. They picked it up. Nannie folded it neatly, and they went indoors with the bit of blue sky.

'It's as soft as velvet and as smooth as silk,' said Joan, feeling it. 'Isn't it lovely? Do you think there's enough to make a sailor a pair of trousers, Nannie?'

'I'm not sure,' said Nannie. 'There doesn't look *quite* enough to me!' She unrolled the bit of sky, and laid it out flat on the floor.

'That bit's enough for one leg, if it's folded over,' she said. 'And that bit, folded the other way, would be almost enough for the other leg. And there's a bit for the top of the trousers too. Dear me, I'm not sure if there's enough!'

'Oh, Nannie, does that mean it won't

be fine this afternoon?' said Joan sadly.

'I'm afraid so,' said Nannie. 'There *must* be enough to make a whole pair of trousers, you know.'

'Nannie, there's enough for trousers for a *small* sailor,' said Harry eagerly. 'Don't you think so? I once saw quite a small sailor, and I'm sure this bit of sky would be big enough for *him*.'

'Well – perhaps there *is* enough for a small sailor!' said Nannie, thinking hard. 'Yes, I believe there would be. That's all right then – the weather will be fine this afternoon. Now, we must send this bit of sky back again.'

Nannie took the blue sky to the window. She opened the window and shot the sky out into the wind. The wind took hold of it and blew it away. Up, up, up it went until it reached the clouds. It squeezed itself between them, and there it shone, a nice little bit of blue sky! It was most extraordinary.

The dinner-bell rang. 'Good gracious, dinner already!' said Nannie. 'Go and wash your hands and brush your hair, both of you!'

Off they went, excited and happy. What a lovely bit of magic they had seen that morning! They ate their dinner quickly, wondering and wondering if what Nannie said was true – that the weather really would clear up and be fine.

And do you know, after their rest, which they always had until quarter-past two, the clouds were almost gone!

The little bit of blue sky had got bigger and bigger and BIGGER – and now there were hardly any clouds, but blue sky everywhere!

'It's true then, it's true!' cried Joan in delight. 'Look at the lovely blue sky and warm sun! We can go out and play Red Indians all the afternoon!'

So out they went and had a lovely time. They *were* so pleased, and they told all their friends about it.

'*We'll* watch the sky next time we want fine weather too!' said their friends. 'It's a splendid thing to know that if there's enough blue sky to make a sailor a pair of trousers, then the weather will be fine!'

Did you know that? Do watch and see, will you, because you'll be so pleased if you find it is really true.

7

Ellen's Adventure

All the school children were excited because the Duchess of Fairholm was coming to open their Sale of Work – a real, live Duchess that everyone loved. What fun!

The children did their best work. The girls made some beautiful nightdress cases and babies' frocks. The boys hammered away in the carpentry room and made some fine stools and tables – and secretly every boy and girl hoped that the Duchess might buy his or her work. Oh, how glorious it would be to go home and tell everyone that the Duchess had chosen something you had made!

Mary's nightdress case was blue with beautiful stitches. Hilda's was yellow. Winnie had made a frock for a year-old baby with little tucks round the bottom. Susan had knitted a blue coat. John had made a stool, very firm and solid. Harry had made a low table, and had polished it till it shone like a mirror. Wilfrid had made a bookshelf with two curly ends. Really, the things that the little school had made were very good indeed.

Ellen had made an apron. It was very gay with yellow flowers all over it and a bright green border round the bottom. The teacher had told her to be sure and leave enough for the apron strings when she had cut it out – and do you know, Ellen forgot! So when she came to do the strings, there was no yellow or green stuff left.

'What shall I do?' she asked the teacher.

'Well, Ellen, that was careless of you,' said Miss White, the teacher. 'You have made the apron very long, instead of nice and short - and have no stuff left for even very short strings. You will have to go to the rag-bag and see if there is any stuff over from someone else.'

Ellen was upset. She had sewn her apron very beautifully - and now it would be spoilt by having strings that didn't match. She went to the rag-bag and rummaged through it. She found a long piece of black stuff - and that was the only piece long enough for strings. So Ellen had to make black strings to

her yellow and green apron.

She had finished it by the great day – and arranged it with all the other work on a long table, for the Duchess to see. Ellen folded the strings underneath because she was ashamed of them. She put her apron right at the very back, out of sight. It would be dreadful if the Duchess unfolded it and saw the strings that didn't match!

'Be at school promptly at two o'clock,' said Miss White, on the morning of the Sale of Work Day. 'The Duchess arrives at half-past two.'

So Ellen made sure to start off early that afternoon, nicely washed and brushed, and in her best frock. She lived three miles from school, so she had a bicycle. She was very glad it wasn't raining!

She was riding along the country lane from her home, when she saw a car coming towards her. It was a green-and-silver car, very shiny and bright. It stopped by her, and the lady at the wheel leaned out.

'Little girl! Is this the way to Pinney village?'

'Oh, no!' said Ellen. 'It's the other way.'

'Oh, thank you,' said the lady, and she began to turn her car round - but a dreadful thing happened. The back wheels slipped into the ditch at the side of the road! The lady couldn't get her car out of the ditch, and she beckoned to Ellen again.

'Is there a garage near here that could send a man to help?' she asked.

'There's one two miles away,' said Ellen. 'But I don't know how you'd get there unless you walked. There isn't a telephone near here either.'

'Oh dear!' said the lady in dismay. 'Little girl, do you think *you* could ride

to the garage for me, and tell the man I want his help at once?'

'Well,' said Ellen, 'it's in the wrong direction for me. I'm supposed to be at school at two o'clock this afternoon.'

'Oh dear, oh dear, whatever shall I do!' sighed the lady, and she looked so unhappy that Ellen made up her mind to help her. She would miss the Duchess opening the Sale of Work - and Miss White might be cross with her - but Mother always said, 'Help where you can,' so perhaps she had better do what she could.

'I'll go for you!' she said, jumping on her bicycle. Off she went, and soon arrived at Tom Brown's garage. She gave the message, and rode off again. Tom Brown passed her on his motor bicycle and waved. Ellen waved back, and pedalled on to school.

She was late, and Miss White scolded her.

'The Duchess will be here any moment,' she said. 'You might have missed her altogether, Ellen. Very naughty of you!'

Just at that minute up drove a car - green-and-silver - and out of it jumped - the lady that Ellen had helped. Just imagine that! She was the Duchess herself, and Ellen hadn't known it. The lady came up the school steps and shook hands with Miss White.

'I'm a minute late,' she said smiling at the children. 'My car was stuck in a ditch, and if it hadn't been for a kind little girl who helped me, I should have been in the ditch still!'

She looked round at the children and

saw Ellen, who was blushing very red.
'Oh, there's the little girl!' she said, and she walked right up to Ellen. 'You must shake hands with me dear, for you were a very good friend to me!'

Ellen was so pleased and proud. Miss White stared in surprise. So that was why Ellen was late – she had helped the Duchess!

Then the Sale of Work was declared open by the Duchess, and she went to see all the children's work. She turned to Miss White and said, 'I must really buy what Ellen has made, to remind me of a kind and helpful little girl.'

Ellen felt her heart stop still. Oh, that apron with the black strings that didn't match! Now the Duchess would see it, and perhaps she would laugh, or say, 'Dear me! How odd! I don't think I'll buy that after all!'

'Where's your apron, Ellen?' said Miss White, looking for it. Ellen silently picked it out from the back. The Duchess shook it out and exclaimed in delight:

'Green and yellow! My very favourite colours. And oh! look at the black strings! How very smart! Just what everyone is wearing! I shall certainly buy *this* apron! It will do nicely for me to wear when I do the flowers each morning. How much is it? Only fifty pence? Oh, that's absurd – I shall pay a pound for it!'

Well, you should have seen Ellen's face! She was so surprised and pleased and excited. She folded up the apron and packed it neatly in paper.

She was quite the heroine of the afternoon, and her mother, who was there, was *so* proud of her! She kissed her when they got ready to go home, after a most thrilling tea, and said, 'What did I always say! Help where you can! And you did, and had a fine reward. I *am* so pleased, Ellen!'

So was Ellen. She often thinks of the pretty Duchess wearing her green-and-yellow apron with the odd black strings!

8

The Big Juicy Carrot

One fine morning, Bobtail, the rabbit, met Long-ears, the hare, and they set off together, talking about this and that.

They stopped by a hedge and lay quiet, for they could hear a cart passing. Bobtail peeped through and saw that it was a farm-cart, laden with carrots and turnips. How his mouth watered!

And then, just as the cart passed where the two animals were crouching, a wheel ran over a great stone, and the jerk made a big, juicy, red carrot fall from the cart to the ground. The hare and the rabbit looked at it in great delight.

When the cart had gone out of sight

The Big Juicy Carrot

the two of them hurried into the lane. Bobtail picked up the carrot. Long-ears spoke eagerly:

'We both saw it at once. We must share it!'

'Certainly!' said Bobtail. 'I will break it in half!'

So he broke the carrot in half - but although each piece measured the same, one bit was the thick top part of the carrot, and the other was the thin bottom part. Bobtail picked up the top part - but Long-ears stopped him.

'One piece is bigger than the other,' he said. 'There is no reason why *you* should have the bigger piece, cousin.'

'And no reason why *you* should, either!' said the rabbit crossly.

'Give it to me!' squealed the hare.

'Certainly *not!*' said the rabbit. They each glared at the other, but neither dared to do any more.

'We had better ask someone to judge between us,' said the hare, at last. 'Whom shall we ask?'

Bobtail looked all round, but he could see no one but Neddy the donkey, peering over the hedge at them.

'There isn't anyone in sight except stupid old Neddy,' he said. 'It's not much good asking *him*. He has no brains to speak of!'

'That's true,' said Long-ears. 'He's an old stupid, everyone knows that. But who else is there to ask?'

'No one,' said Bobtail. 'Well, come on. Let's take the carrot to the donkey and ask him to choose which of us shall have the larger piece.'

So they ran through the hole in the hedge and went up to Neddy. He had heard every word they said and was

not at all pleased to be thought so stupid.

The two creatures told him what they wanted.

'If I am so stupid as you think, I wonder you want me to judge,' said Neddy, blinking at them.

'Well, you will have to do,' said the rabbit. 'Now tell us - how are we to know which of us shall have the bigger piece?'

'I can soon put that right for you, even with *my* poor brain!' said Neddy. He took the larger piece in his mouth and bit off the end.

'Perhaps that will have made them the same size!' he said, crunching up the juicy bit of carrot he had bitten off.

But no - he had bitten off such a big

piece that now the piece that *had* been the larger one was smaller than the other!

'Soon put *that* right!' said Neddy, and he picked up the second piece. He bit a large piece off that one, and then dropped it. But now it was much smaller than the first piece!

The hare and the rabbit watched in alarm. This was dreadful!

'Stop, Neddy!' said Long-ears. 'Give us what is left. You have no right to crunch up our carrot!'

'Well, I am only trying to help you!' said Neddy indignantly. 'Wait a moment. Perhaps *this* time I'll make the pieces equal.'

He took another bite at a piece of carrot - oh dear, such a big bite this time! The two animals were in despair.

'Give us the rest!' they begged. 'Do not eat any more!'

'Well,' said Neddy, looking at the last two juicy pieces, and keeping his foot on them so that the two animals could not get them, 'what about my payment for troubling to settle your quarrel? What will you give me for that?'

'Nothing at all!' cried Long-ears.

'What! Nothing at all?' said Neddy, in anger. 'Very well, then - I shall take my own payment!'

And with that he put his head down and took up the rest of the carrot! Chomp-chomp-chomp! He crunched it all up with great enjoyment.

'Thanks!' he said to Long-ears and Bobtail. 'That was very nice. I'm obliged to you.'

He cantered away to the other side of the field, and as he went, he brayed loudly with laughter. The two big-eyed creatures looked at one another.

'Bobtail,' said Long-ears, 'do you think that donkey was as stupid as we thought he was?'

'No, I don't,' groaned Bobtail. 'He was much cleverer than we were - and you know Long-ears, if one of us had been sensible, we would *both* now be nibbling carrot - instead of seeing that stupid donkey chewing it all up!'

They ran off - Bobtail to his hole and Long-ears to the field where he had his home. As for Neddy, he put his head over the wall and told his friend, the brown horse, all about that big juicy carrot.

You *should* have heard them laugh!

9

Little Tom Taylor

Little Tom Taylor was only three, but he knew every animal and bird in the farmyard. And they all knew and loved Tom Taylor.

He took fresh carrots to the two donkeys. He found green apples for the old brown cart-horse. He brought bones to the farm-dogs, and put down saucers of milk for the four cats. He fed the hens and the ducks, and he took scraps to the pigs.

Tom Taylor lived on his father's farm. It was a big one, and the main road, with its buses and cars, ran along one side of it. Tom Taylor's mother was always afraid that the little boy might get into the main road and be run over.

But Tom Taylor's father wired up the hedge that ran along by the main road,

so little Tom Taylor couldn't g
it. Then his mother felt quite s
him, and she let him go wher
wanted to on the farm.

'Here comes Tom Taylor!' grunted the pigs as they saw him coming with a dish of scraps.

'Here's our little Tom Taylor!' said the hens and the ducks, with loud clucks and quacks, as he came with a basket of corn.

'Dear old Tom Taylor!' said the sheep, looking through the bars of their

gate as the little boy ran to and fro about his work.

'Thank you, Tom Taylor!' said Brownie, the old cart-horse, nibbling the apple that the little boy brought out from his pocket to give to him.

Now Tom Taylor loved the farm, but he loved something else too. He loved the main road, with all its cars and buses. Often he went to the wired-up hedge and watched the busy traffic rushing by his father's farm. And how he wished he could get right on to the road and see everything more closely! But he couldn't get through the wire.

And then one day a man pushing a barrow was squeezed into the hedge by a passing car, and his barrow ran into the wire netting and tore a hole. The man pulled his barrow out again and went on his way – but the hole was left behind in the wire, and Tom Taylor saw it.

It was a very scratchy sort of hole. Tom Taylor bent the scratchy bits back here and there, and then he felt sure that the hole was big enough for him to squeeze through. He would be in the road then and could see the big buses very close.

So he squeezed through and stood in the road below, watching all the cars. Then he thought he would go to the other side and watch from there - and dear me, little Tom Taylor nearly got run over by a great, big black car!

Now when tea-time came, and the animals looked for Tom Taylor to come with their tea, they couldn't see him.

Where was he? His own tea-bell rang, but no Tom Taylor went running in.

'He hasn't brought our corn,' clucked the hens.

'He didn't give us any carrots,' said the donkeys.

'He forgot our milk!' said the cats.

And then one of the cows in the field away by the main road began to moo excitedly.

'What does that cow say?' asked the ducks.

'Oh! She says that Tom Taylor is in the road!' cried the hens. 'Cluck, cluck, cluck! Go and tell the dogs.'

So the ducks told the farm-dogs, and the dogs were very upset. They ran to tell their mistress, Tom Taylor's mother, but she couldn't understand their barks and told them to be quiet. She didn't know that they were saying, 'Wuff, wuff, Mistress! Our Tom Taylor is in the road and may be run over.'

So the dogs ran to tell the donkeys, and the two donkeys swished their tails and wondered what to do. 'If only we were in the main-road field we could bray to Tom Taylor and tell him to come back,' they said. 'But how did he get through the wire?'

'Moo-oo-oo!' bellowed the cows. 'There is a big hole there. That's how he got out.'

'We'd better tell Brownie, the old carthorse,' said the two donkeys. 'He is old and wise and will know what to do. We cannot have any harm coming to little kind Tom Taylor!'

So they ran to the old horse, who was standing all alone at the end of the cows' field, eating grass and wondering why he had not seen Tom Taylor that afternoon.

'Old horse!' called the two donkeys, galloping up and looking at him over the hedge. 'Tom Taylor is in the road. Do you think he will be run over?'

'Oh my! Oh my!' neighed the big cart-horse, and he galloped away to the far-off hedge that ran along beside the main road. He looked over it - and there was Tom Taylor, looking at all the cars and buses, on the opposite side of the road.

The horse was just going to neigh when he thought that perhaps Tom Taylor might come rushing across the road to pat him on the nose, if he heard him - and as he was so little he might not look to see if anything was coming and he would be knocked down. So he couldn't neigh to Tom Taylor.

Could he get through the hole in the wire? The old horse found the hole, but he knew he could never get *his* big body through it. Whatever could he do?

'Well, I must take a big run and see if I can jump right over the hedge!' thought the clever old horse. So he ran back a good way, galloped straight at the high hedge, rose into the air, and jumped right over it, not even his heels touching the top.

'Crash!' He landed in the road, and ran across to little Tom Taylor, who was most surprised to see him.

'Nei-ei-eigh! Come home to tea!' said the horse. But Tom Taylor didn't want to! He just stood there beside the old horse and looked at two big buses rumbling by. Then the horse bent down his head, took hold of little Tom Taylor's trouser-belt with his strong teeth, lifted him up by that and walked slowly across the road with him, making all the cars stop.

But he couldn't jump over the hedge with Tom Taylor, for the little boy was heavy, and, besides, he was struggling to get down.

So the horse trotted down the main road, still carrying Tom Taylor by his belt. All the way down he went until he came to the lane that led to the farmhouse. Up it he went and came to the front door. He knocked it with his foot.

Tom Taylor's mother opened the door. The old horse put the little boy down and neighed. *How* surprised his mother was!

'Tom Taylor! Where have you been?' she cried. 'Oh, you naughty little boy,

I've been looking everywhere for you. Where were you?'

'I was in the road watching the cars,' said Tom Taylor, 'and Brownie came and fetched me away. He's naughty.'

'He's not. He's the most sensible horse in the world!' cried Tom Taylor's mother. 'Come in, Brownie, and you shall have a sugar-lump!'

And do you know, for the first time in his life the old horse walked down the hall and into the dining-room, where he had the biggest lump of sugar out of the basin! You simply cannot imagine how pleased he was!

10

Biggitty and the Green Hen

Once Biggitty the brownie did a dreadful thing. He crept through a hole in Dame Clucker's fence, slipped inside her hen-house, and stole an egg! Nobody saw him. Nobody knew.

But when Biggitty got back home and looked at the egg, he got a shock! It was bright green! Now the brownie knew it must be an enchanted egg of some sort, and he wondered what to do.

'I'll boil it!' he said. 'If it's boiled it can't do any harm. If it tastes nice I'll have it for my tea.'

So he popped it into a saucepan of boiling water - but after a minute the egg began to sing loudly, 'Wheeee-ee, wheeee-ee!' And, before Biggitty's astonished eyes it burst with a loud pop - and out sprang a tiny, green hen, complete to the last feather in her tail!

'Oooh!' said Biggitty, and made a grab at it. But the hen dodged neatly to one side. She flew up to the beam in the

ceiling and preened her feathers, keeping a sharp eye on Biggitty.

Now Biggitty was not only a dishonest little brownie, but he was also untruthful and not very clean. So the little green hen was not very lucky in her owner. She stayed up in the rafters, watching everything. She saw that Biggitty's hands were dirty. She saw that his nails were simply black. She noticed that his hair had not been brushed. There wasn't a thing she didn't see!

Biggitty didn't at all like the way the little green hen watched him. He glared at her, and said, 'Stare all you like! That won't do me any harm. Wait till I get hold of you!'

'Clucka-lucka-luck!' said the hen, and scratched the back of her head thoughtfully.

A knock came at the door and a pixie put his head in. 'Coming out for a walk, Biggitty?' he called. Before Biggitty could answer, a voice came from the rafters:

'Biggitty hasn't washed behind his ears this morning.'

The pixie stared at Biggitty, laughed and went away. Biggitty was furious. He caught up a broom and tried to sweep the green hen off the beam. But she dodged away and he swept down a great string of onions, that fell round his neck.

'Wait till I get you!' said Biggitty to the clucking hen.

The baker came to the door and looked in. 'Any bread to-day?'

'Cluck-a-cluck! Biggitty's nails could grow potatoes!' shouted the little green hen. The baker took a look at Biggitty's nails, gave a shudder, and went away. Biggitty could hardly say a word, he was so angry. He shut the door and the windows, and fetched his step-ladder. He meant to get that little green hen down! But she flew up the chimney, found a nook there out of the smoke, and stayed there, clucking loudly. And nothing Biggitty could do would get her down. She didn't seem to mind heat or smoke at all.

Dame Twiddle came to call. She sat down on a chair and asked Biggitty if he was well.

'Clucka-lucka-luck!' screamed the hen up the chimney. 'His teeth aren't well because he never cleans them.'

'Dear me!' said Dame Twiddle. 'Is this a new pet of yours, Biggitty?'

'No,' said Biggitty angrily. 'Please go, Dame Twiddle. I'm busy to-day.'

'Yes! He has got to brush his hair and wash his hands!' said the voice in the chimney. 'Clucka-lucka-luck!'

Dame Twiddle took a quick look at Biggitty's untidy hair and dirty hands and chuckled.

'Well, you've got some good advice!' she said. 'I should take it, Biggitty!'

As soon as she was gone, Biggitty poured some water on the fire. It sizzled loudly and clouds of smoke poured out into the room. Then Biggitty stamped on the embers and what do you suppose he did? He began to climb up the chimney! He MEANT to get that little green hen! Yes, he did!

Up he climbed and up, and came at last to where the little green hen was cosy in her nook. She pecked him, but he took hold of her. He climbed down again, put her into a basket, and took her next door to Dame Clucker.

Dame Clucker opened the door.

'Good afternoon,' said Biggitty. 'I've brought one of your hens back. She must have escaped through the fence.'

'Dear me, that's very, very good of you,' said Dame Clucker, in surprise. She took the basket - but the little green hen flew out and was away in the air before either the brownie or the old dame could catch her.

'Well, well!' said Dame Clucker. 'She's gone! Take an egg from my henhouse, Biggitty, in return for bringing me back the hen.'

'Oh no, thank you!' said Biggitty hurriedly. He had had quite enough of Dame Clucker's eggs! He ran home in glee. Aha! He had got rid of that wretched bird, and earned a good mark for himself from Dame Clucker!

He set his tea, humming. The postman brought him a letter, and stayed for a chat. Suddenly a voice came from the chimney:

'Clucka-lucka-luck! Biggitty has two big holes in his stockings. I saw his toes poking through when he changed his shoes.'

The postman giggled and went out laughing. Biggitty turned pale with fright and then red with anger. So that horrid, horrid green hen had come back again! He went to the chimney and looked up.

'Are you up there *again?*' he called.

The little green hen scraped about and dislodged a lot of soot that went flying down the chimney and covered Biggitty from head to foot. What a sight he looked!

'Biggitty is very black and dirty! Clucka-lucka-luck!' said the hen brightly.

So Biggitty was! He stood storming at the hen. Then he went off to have a bath. He soaped himself well. He washed behind his ears. He cleaned his teeth and his nails. He brushed his wet hair till it lay smooth and shining. He put on clean clothes, for the soot had

got into every corner of his other clothes.

Just as he had finished, there came a knock at the door. Tiptoe, the little pixie, looked in.

'Oh!' she said, when she saw Biggitty, 'how smart you look!'

'Clucka-lucka-luck!' screamed the little green hen in the chimney. 'He has washed his hands. He has washed behind his ears. He has cleaned his nails. He has brushed his hair. He has no holes in his stockings.'

Biggitty blushed - but Tiptoe looked at him admiringly. 'What a clean brownie you must be!' she said. 'I will come and have tea with you on Saturday!'

She skipped off. Biggitty *was* pleased to think that such a pretty little pixie should say nice things to him. He went and admired himself in the glass.

'Clucka-lucka-luck!' said the voice in the chimney. 'Biggitty is very conceited! He stares at himself in the glass!'

Biggitty was going to poke a broom up the chimney to try and get down the hen when he stopped himself and thought for a moment.

'No,' he said. 'That bird is only telling the truth. I was pleased just now when it told the truth and said nice things. It is my own fault if it says nasty things! I will see that it only has nice things to say! Aha! That will make it feel blue!'

So Biggitty turned over a new leaf

and became a clean and good little brownie. The green hen found nothing but good things to say, and soon she had so little fear of Biggitty that she hopped down the chimney and sat on the arm of his chair beside him.

Now she is his pet! She takes seed from his hand, and lets him stroke her. And when Tiptoe, the pixie, comes to tea the little green hen has a fine time, for they both spoil her thoroughly.

She only says nice things now, and if ever you go to see Biggitty, don't be surprised if you hear a voice from the chimney or the ceiling, will you - saying, 'Biggitty washed his neck well this morning!' Or, 'Biggitty had a bath last night! Clucka-lucka-luck!'

11

Susy-Ann's Clock

Susy-Ann was lazy and slow. She was late for school, she was late for dinner, she was late for bed. She was late for everything!

And do you know what she said

when people scolded her for being late? She said, 'Well, I couldn't help it. It was my clock's fault, because it is always going slow!'

Now, when the clock heard Susy-Ann saying this, it felt very angry. For one thing it never did go slow, but kept the most perfect time - and for another thing the clock hated to hear anyone telling untruths.

The clock belonged to Susy-Ann. It was a very pretty one, and hung on the wall. It was green, with big figures all round its face, and two black hands, one long and one short.

It grumbled away to itself when it heard what Susy-Ann said. 'Tick-tock, tick-tock, what a shock, what a shock; tock-tick-tock-tick, if only Susy-Ann were quick!'

But always Susy-Ann was slow and lazy and always she made the same excuse, 'My clock is slow.'

And then the clock made up its mind to play a few tricks on Susy-Ann! Instead of keeping good time, or of

going slow, it would go fast! Yes, that's what it would do! Then Susy-Ann would be surprised to find that she would have to hurry, hurry, hurry!

So the next morning, when the hands should have pointed to half-past seven – time for Susy-Ann to get up – they ran on to eight o'clock! And when Susy-Ann yawned and thought she really *had* better get up, the clock struck eight!

'Gracious!' said Susy-Ann, sitting up at once. 'It can't be eight! I'll have no breakfast! I'll never be in time for school. I must get up quickly! Oh dear, oh dear, I'd no idea it was so late!'

She dressed more quickly than she had ever dressed in her life before. She shot downstairs - and there was her mother, just putting the breakfast-things on the table.

'My goodness, you *are* early!' she said to Susy-Ann. 'It's not eight o'clock yet!'

'But my clock struck eight ages ago!' said Susy-Ann. 'I'll go back to my room and tell you what the right time is, Mother.'

She ran back; but the clock had put itself right as soon as the little girl had left the room, and its hands pointed to the right time - ten minutes to eight. Susy-Ann was *most* astonished!

She had her breakfast and then her mother told her to go and make her bed, wash her hands, and brush her hair again. So she went to her room. But how she dawdled! She read a book. She played a game of snakes and ladders by herself till the clock got really angry. So, very quietly, it ran its hands round its face till they pointed to nine o'clock! It struck loudly nine times.

'Oooh!' squealed Susy-Ann in a fright. 'I shall be later than ever at school!' She put her hat on, caught up her coat, and rushed off without even saying good-bye to her mother. She forgot her biscuits for lunch and forgot her pencil-box, and she forgot to take back the book she had borrowed from school!

The clock laughed. It sent its hands back to the right time, which was twenty minutes to nine. Susy-Ann would be *very* early at school for once!

She was! She got there at a quarter to nine, very much out of breath. Nobody was there. She was the first. The school door was shut.

'How funny!' said Susy-Ann in astonishment. 'Where's everybody?'

The other children soon came. How surprised they were to see Susy-Ann there first!

But Susy-Ann got into trouble because she had forgotten her book and her pencil-box. She was sad at eleven o'clock, too, because she had no biscuits to eat.

When her teacher scolded her for forgetting her book and her pencils, Susy-Ann spoke up. 'My clock must have been fast this morning,' she said. 'It sent me off in a dreadful hurry, and I hadn't time to remember my things.'

'Really, Susy-Ann!' said the teacher. 'You blame your clock for everything!

First you say it is slow - and now you say it is fast.'

Susy-Ann ran home to dinner. She went to look at her clock. It said exactly the same as the one in the dining-room - one o'clock. That was all right then. It wasn't fast and it wasn't slow.

'Dinner is at a quarter-past one, Susy,' her mother called. 'Wash your hands and be ready.'

Susy-Ann didn't wash her hands. She began to read a book. She read and she read. The clock began to feel very angry again. What a lazy, slow little girl! The clock quietly ran its hands

round its face - and do you know, it pointed to two o'clock! It struck two, very loudly, 'Dong! Dong!'

Susy-Ann gave a scream. 'Oh! Oh! Whatever am I thinking of? I must have read for ages - and now it is school-time. I haven't time for dinner. I haven't time for anything. It's handicraft this afternoon, and I shan't be allowed to do it if I'm late!'

And do you know what she did? She put on her hat, ran straight downstairs and out of the door, and went off to school without any dinner! Her mother called her, but she wouldn't answer.

'Whatever *is* the matter with Susy-Ann?' wondered her mother. 'Where can she have gone to? Just as I am getting her dinner ready, too! Naughty little girl.'

The clock grinned to itself, and put

its hands right - they pointed to a quarter-past one. Susy-Ann had had to hurry herself that day! What fun!

Poor Susy-Ann! She found six children at school having their dinner with the teacher. They were all very surprised to see Susy.

'Why have you come back, Susy-Ann?' asked the teacher. 'Surely you haven't had your dinner yet?'

'Well, my clock said two o'clock,' said Susy-Ann in astonishment.

'It's wrong then,' said the teacher, looking at her watch. 'It is only twenty-five past one.'

Susy-Ann went red. How silly the teacher must think her! She ran back home again. Her mother was very angry with her.

'Susy, what do you mean by running off like that just when your dinner was ready?' she cried.

'Well, my clock struck two, and I thought I was very late,' said Susy-Ann.

'How could it strike two, when it is

Susy-Ann's Clock

only just striking half-past one now!' said her mother. 'Listen!'

Susy listened. The clock had struck one, sure enough. She looked into her bedroom and saw that it was saying half-past one. It was really very extraordinary.

Susy-Ann was very thoughtful as she ate her dinner. She was sure there was something funny about her clock. Perhaps it was playing tricks on her. Perhaps it was punishing her for always being slow and blaming it on the clock.

After her dinner she went to look at the clock. It said five minutes to two. School began at a quarter-past.

'I'll just pretend to be very slow, and see what that clock does,' said Susy-Ann to herself. So she pretended to dawdle round - and the clock became angry again. It slyly sent on its hands to a quarter-past two - but Susy-Ann saw them moving.

'I saw you, I saw you!' she cried. 'You wicked clock!'

'Tick-tock, tock-tick, well you really should be quick,' said the clock sulkily.

'I will, if you'll promise not to play any tricks on me,' said Susy-Ann. 'I know I'm slow, but I *can* be quick - only please, please don't tell me the wrong time, Clock, because you'll make me miss my dinner and my tea, and do all sorts of funny things.'

'Tick-tock, tock-tick, I'll be good if you are quick,' promised the clock, and it sent its hands round to ten to three so that it looked exactly as if it were smiling. Then it put itself right, and struck two o'clock.

And now the clock behaves itself - and so does Susy-Ann. Nobody can guess what has changed Susy-Ann - and I'm sure they wouldn't believe her if she told them!

12
Susie and Her Shadow

Once a very funny thing happened to Susie. She was sitting in the sunshine, reading a book, when she saw a small pixie running by her with a big pair of scissors.

Susie was so surprised to see a pixie that at first she couldn't say a word. She just stared and stared. The pixie spoke first.

'Hallo!' he said. 'I suppose you don't really want your shadow, do you?'

'Whatever do you mean?' cried Susie.

'Well,' said the pixie, 'I'm just asking you if you want your shadow. It's no use to you. It would be *very* useful to me, if you'd let me have it.'

'But what do you want a shadow for?' asked Susie.

'Well,' said the pixie, whispering, 'you see, it's like this. I know a spell to make a magic cloak. If anyone puts on this magic cloak they will not be seen – they will be quite invisible. And I *do* want a magic cloak!'

'But what's a shadow got to do with a magic cloak?' asked Susie in surprise.

'You *are* stupid,' said the pixie impatiently. 'The magic cloak is made of somebody's shadow, of course. That is why I want your shadow.'

'But I want my shadow too,' said Susie.

'Now don't be silly and selfish,' said the pixie, opening and shutting his big scissors. 'What use is your shadow to you? Does it play with you?'

'No,' said Susie.

'Does it help you to do your lessons?' said the pixie.

'No,' said Susie.

'Does it keep you warm?' said the pixie.

'Of course not,' said Susie.

'Well, then!' cried the pixie. 'What's the use of it? None at all! You might just as well let me have it.'

'Why don't you cut your *own* shadow?' said Susie suddenly. 'If my shadow is no use to me, then yours is certainly no use to *you*! You CAN'T have my

Susie and Her Shadow

shadow, Pixie, so now you know.'

Then the pixie fell into a tremendous rage and stamped about and shouted. Susie was a bit afraid at first, and then he looked so funny that she couldn't help laughing.

'Oh! So you're laughing at me, are you?' cried the little fellow in a rage. 'Then I'll steal your shadow without waiting for you to say yes!'

And with that he opened his big scissors and began to cut all round poor Susie's shadow. Of course it didn't hurt her, but it was dreadful to see her pretty purple shadow being cut away behind her. She tried to stop the little pixie, but he was too quick. With three or four snips of his sharp scissors he had cut off the whole of Susie's shadow.

Then he neatly rolled it up, put it over his shoulder, laughed loudly and ran off. Susie ran after him. The pixie ran to a rabbit-burrow and disappeared down it. He was gone.

Susie began to cry. She looked behind her. She had no shadow at all, not even the tiniest one, and it was strange to be without her shadow.

'I don't feel right without my shadow,' she wept. 'And how everyone will laugh at me. They'll call me The Girl Without a Shadow!'

She was so busy crying and wiping her eyes that she did not see a fat little brownie looking at her from his house in a tree. He had opened his door, which was cut in the trunk, and was looking very puzzled.

'Little girl! Whatever's the matter?'

he called at last. 'You are making such a noise that I can't hear my radio.'

Susie had already had so many surprises that she hardly felt astonished at all to see a brownie looking out of a tree-house at her. She wiped her eyes and answered him.

'Well, *you'd* cry too, if you'd just had your shadow cut off by a mean little pixie who wanted to make a magic cloak with it!' said the little girl.

'Good gracious!' said the brownie, stepping out of his tree and looking closely at Susie. 'You are quite right. You haven't a shadow. Well, well, well!'

'It isn't well at all,' said Susie. 'It's perfectly horrid. I simply don't know what to do. The pixie went down this rabbit-hole, and I'm too big to follow him.'

'I can help you,' said the brownie. 'Come inside my tree-house and you can go down to my cellars. They lead into the passage to the pixie's home, just near that rabbit-burrow.'

'Oh, thank you,' said Susie. She

climbed into the tree-house after the brownie. She had hardly time to see what it was like, because the brownie took her so quickly down some winding steps right to his cellars. He opened a door there, and Susie peered out into a dark passage.

'Where do we go from here?' she whispered.

'Follow me,' said the brownie. He led the way down the passage till they came to a door marked 'Mister Pixie Podge.'

'This is where he lives,' said the brownie. He hit the door with his fist and it flew open. Susie stared inside.

She saw a small room, just like a

cave. From the rocky ceiling hung a bright lantern. Underneath it sat the naughty pixie, sewing away at Susie's purple shadow. He looked up in surprise as the door flew open.

'So you stole this little girl's shadow, did you?' said the brownie in a fierce voice. 'Another of your bits of mischief, Podge! Give it back to her at once.'

'Shan't!' said the pixie, and in a trice he flung the purple shadow round his shoulders like a cloak. At once he disappeared!

'There! He's gone!' said Susie. 'He told me that a shadow would make a magic cloak, and it was true. Now what are we to do?'

'We can't get your shadow back, that's certain,' said the brownie, puzzled. Then he grinned. He caught up the pixie's large pair of scissors, which were on a nearby table. He ran to the other side of the lantern where a blue shadow lay on the floor.

'Look!' said the brownie. 'The pixie has disappeared all right – but his shadow hasn't! I'll cut it off, and give it to you.'

Before the pixie could run away the brownie had snipped three times with the scissors - and the pixie's shadow was cut off. The brownie rolled it up and gave it to the surprised little girl.

'There you are!' he said. 'He took *your* shadow - now you've got his!'

'But how can I put it on me?' asked Susie in dismay. 'I can't possibly!'

'Dear, dear! what a fusser you are!' said the brownie. 'Come back with me and I'll see what I can do for you.'

So, leaving the little underground room, where they could hear the pixie crying, although they could not see him, the two went back to the tree-house. The brownie found a work-basket, threaded a needle with blue cotton, and then took the shadow from Susie. He made her stand up, and then he neatly fitted the shadow's feet to her own feet. He quickly sewed it to her shoes with such tiny stitches that Susie couldn't possibly see them.

'There you are!' he said. 'That's done.'

Then he suddenly began to laugh. He laughed and laughed, and Susie got quite cross with him.

'Whatever's the matter?' she said.

'Well,' said the brownie, giggling, 'well, little girl, just look. You've got a pixie's shadow instead of your own. See the pointed ears! Oh, it's very funny!'

Susie looked round at her shadow. The brownie was perfectly right. She had a pixie shadow! Although she was a little girl, her shadow was that of a fairy. Susie suddenly felt very pleased.

'I'm glad,' she said. 'I'm glad. I know this isn't a dream now, because I've only got to look at my shadow and see a fairy's shadow, and I'll know it's all true! Oh, what fun!'

And off she skipped home, her pixie shadow following her and skipping too. I think she's lucky, don't you? Do you know a Susie? Well, have a look at her shadow next time you see her, and if it's like a pixie's, you'll know she's the same Susie as the one in this story!

13

The Girl Who Tore Her Books

Anna was a funny little girl. She took great care of her toys, especially her dolls - but, dear me, how naughty she was with her books!

She liked nothing better than to tear the pages into small bits! As soon as she was left alone in the nursery she would take a book from the shelf, sit down on the floor with it, and then find a picture. In two seconds the picture was torn in half! Her mother gave her old newspapers to tear up, but Anna didn't want those. It was books she loved to tear.

And then one day something happened. She was alone in the nursery after tea. There was no light except the firelight that flickered everywhere. Anna crept to the shelf and took down a big nursery-rhyme book that her mother had forbidden her to touch.

She badly wanted to tear up the pictures of the nursery-rhyme folk inside, and throw the pieces over the floor. She opened the book at the page where the Old Woman looked out of her shoe. And just as she was going to tear the shoe in half, a strange feeling came over her.

She felt giddy and shut her eyes. She

opened them and looked at her book – but what was happening? The shoe seemed to be growing right out of the book – it was getting bigger and bigger and bigger! The Old Woman was getting bigger too – her mouth was opening and shutting – Anna could hear her talking!

'Come to bed, children!' she was saying. 'Come to bed! I've got your broth ready for you!'

The shoe became so big that it almost filled the nursery! Then Anna saw crowds of small children running round it, shouting and laughing. The Old Woman clapped her hands and cried loudly, 'Come along, come along!'

Three of the children ran up to Anna, and looked at her.

'What a funny little girl!' they said. 'She doesn't look real! She's made of paper!'

Anna looked down at herself in surprise. She *did* look rather queer! She had gone very, very thin, almost as thin as paper. How strange! She looked as if she had been cut out of a picture-book.

'Mother! Mother! Come and look at this funny little girl!' cried the children. 'Is she a paper girl?'

The Old Woman stepped out of her shoe-house and walked over to where Anna stood. She looked at her in surprise.

'Why, it's the naughty little girl I have so often heard about!' she said. 'She is the one who tears all her nice picture-books to pieces. Something magic has happened. She is made of paper herself now.'

'Oh, Mother, do let's tear her then!' cried the children, dancing round. 'It

The Girl who Tore Her Books

won't hurt her if she's made of paper.'

'It *will* hurt me,' said Anna, crying in fright. 'I know it will. Don't touch me.'

'Oh, do let's try and see!' said a small boy, taking hold of Anna's arm. 'Just let me tear a bit of your arm. You are always tearing up people in books. Now it is your turn.'

Anna jerked away her arm. 'Don't!' she said. 'If you try to tear me, I'll shout for my mother.'

'She isn't here,' said a little girl. 'There's only our Mother here, and she will put you to bed if you make too much noise.'

'Well, I won't be torn up,' said Anna. 'I am not made of paper, though I may look as if I am. I shall go back to my own proper self in a minute, I expect, and if you tear me now I might find myself without an arm or something later on. Leave me alone.'

'But you always tear up your books,' said the little boy, dancing round Anna. 'If you tear paper people, why can't we?'

'I wish I hadn't now,' said poor Anna. 'I'll never do it again!'

A big boy went behind Anna and took hold of her paper dress. There was a sound of tearing, and Anna screamed in fright.

'You've torn my dress! Oh, you've torn my dress! You bad, naughty boy!'

'It's only paper,' grinned the boy. 'Ha, ha! Now I've torn your dress just as you've often torn the dresses of people in books! How do you like it?'

Anna flew at the big boy and slapped his face hard. He yelled out in pain and smacked Anna. She began to cry, and all the other children shouted. The Old Woman came out from her shoe again with a frown on her face. She caught hold of one child after another and pushed them into the shoe.

'You'll get some broth without any bread, and then you'll be whipped and sent to bed!' she grumbled. 'Fighting like that! I'm ashamed of you!'

She caught hold of Anna too, but the little girl, afraid of being made one of the shoe-children, wriggled away. The Old Woman caught hold of her dress - and it tore once again!

Anna was pushed into the shoe with all the other children. She looked about for a way to escape, but the Old Woman shut the shoe-door tightly and locked it. Anna saw another door at the back and ran for it.

'Come back, you naughty girl!' cried the Old Woman - but Anna had opened the door and was running out as fast as she could!

There were some stairs in front of her and she ran down them, panting. At the bottom she bumped into someone, and a voice said, ‘Anna dear! Whatever is the matter?’

It was her mother, just coming up the stairs! Anna stopped and looked round. She was at the bottom of the stairs that led to the nursery! How very strange! She looked down at herself, but it was

dark, and she couldn't see if she was still made of paper.

'Mother! Feel me! Am I made of paper or am I real again?' cried Anna, holding on to her surprised mother.

'Anna, you must have been dreaming,' said her mother, taking her upstairs to the nursery and switching on the light. 'Of course you're not made of paper, darling!'

Anna looked down at herself, and sighed with relief. Yes - she was her own solid, real self again.

Then her mother frowned.

'Oh, Anna, look how you've torn your frock! In two places! However did you do that?'

'Mother, a boy from the shoe tore it, and so did the Old Woman when I ran away,' said Anna.

But of course her mother didn't believe her, and she scolded Anna hard.

'It is very, very naughty of you to spoil that nice frock,' she said. 'You are always tearing books - and if you start tearing frocks too, I shall have to send you to bed each time you do it. I am very angry, Anna.'

Anna began to cry. 'I am not going to tear my books any more,' she said. 'Please believe me, Mother. I promise I won't.'

Well, she didn't. She had to mend her torn frock herself, and it took her one whole morning. And now, when her mother wants to read her nursery rhymes, Anna always turns over the page about the Old Woman and won't let it be read. I am not surprised, are you?

14

The Great Big Snowman

Jane and John ran out into the snow. It lay thick on the ground and was so white that it was quite dazzling in the sunshine.

'Let's build a snowman!' cried Jane. 'We have plenty of time, John. We can make a really big one!'

So they set to work. First they made a big snowball, and then they rolled this all the way down the garden and back. It got bigger and bigger as it rolled along, and when it was big enough the children used it for the snowman's body, building it up higher once they had got it into place.

He was very tall - as tall as the children - and when he had his big, round snowhead on, he was just a bit taller. Really, he was a very grand snowman indeed.

'Daddy! Daddy! Will you lend us an old hat to put on the snowman's head?' called the children, when Daddy looked out of the window.

'I say! What a fine snowman!' said Daddy, in surprise. 'Yes, you can have a hat for him. I'll bring you my old garden hat. It has a hole in it now, so I shan't use it any more. The snowman is welcome to it!'

Daddy brought out the hat, and also an old pair of gardening gloves for the snowman's cold hands. He found some

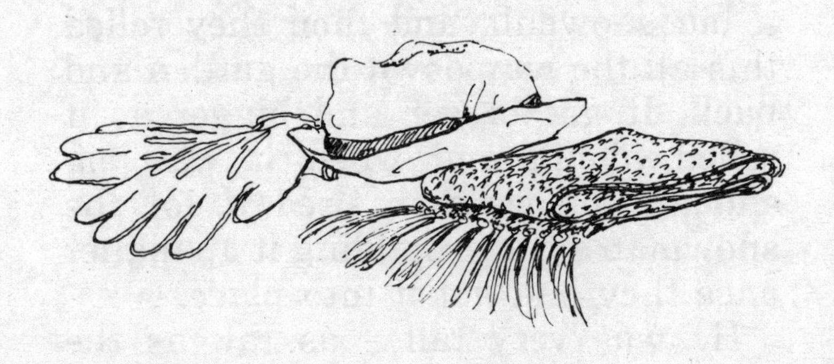

large round stones too, and these the children put all the way down the snowman's body for buttons. He did look grand.

'Mother! Come and look!' shouted the children. So Mother came, and she thought the snowman looked really fine. She gave Jane and John a scarf to put round his neck. It was bright red, so you can guess how grand he looked. The children were delighted with him!

When they went to bed that night, they looked out of the window at him.

There was only a very little moon, so they could not see him very well; he looked like a man standing in the middle of the garden.

'Doesn't he look real now?' said Jane to John. 'Suppose he came alive! Wouldn't it be fun?'

'Snowmen never come alive. Don't be silly, Jane,' said John. The two children hopped into bed and soon fell asleep. Jane dreamt she had gone to a party with a hundred snowmen, and John dreamt he had been turned into a snowman himself and couldn't walk or run.

Now all this time the snowman stood alone in the garden. And, in the middle of the night, two other people came to the garden. They were two burglars, and they had come to steal the silver cups and dishes that the children's father had won playing golf. They crept up the garden path, but suddenly they stopped.

'I say, Bill!' whispered one. 'There's someone in the garden to-night. Look!'

Bill looked to where his friend pointed, and he saw the old snowman, standing quite still in the middle of the lawn. The snowman looked real – like a big man watching them. The two men were frightened.

'Is it the policeman, Jim?' whispered Bill.

'It looks like him,' said Bill. 'Let's hide here till he goes off.'

So the two men hid by the hedge, and kept as still as could be. They watched the snowman, and wondered why the policeman, as they thought, didn't move.

'He *must* be watching for us!' said Bill. 'Let's creep off, Jim. We may be able to get away before he sees us.'

So the two men began to creep down the path. And just at that moment, who should come down the road but the *real* policeman, riding quietly on his bicycle.

The men were so busy watching the snowman that they didn't see or hear the policeman at all. They were creeping out of the front gate when the policeman saw them, and, quick as lightning, he jumped off his bicycle, flashed his light into their faces, and recognised them.

'Oho, Bill and Jim!' he said. 'And what may you be doing here, I'd like to know?'

He blew his whistle loudly, and

round the corner came another policeman on a bicycle, and the children's father also came running out. The men were caught, and the policeman told them they must go to the police station with him.

'We weren't doing anything,' said Bill sulkily. 'And anyway, there was a policeman watching us from the grass over there. *He'll* tell you we didn't go into the house or do anything we shouldn't. Talk about policemen! This road seems full of them to-night!'

'A policeman on our grass!' said Daddy, in astonishment. 'Whatever do you mean?'

'Well, who's that over there, then?' said Bill, and he pointed to the snowy lawn.

The policemen flashed their lamps over the grass, and there stood the old snowman, in Daddy's hat and Mummy's scarf.

'Stars and moon, it's only a snowman!' said the two burglars, in disgust. 'To think we were scared by that! Why, we thought it was a policeman!'

Daddy laughed. 'The children will be pleased to hear that their snowman saved us from being robbed tonight!' he said.

'Yes sir,' said the two policemen,

grinning. 'Come on now, you two men. We want you for many robberies, and we're glad to get you. We're grateful to the snowman for helping us to catch you!'

Off they went - and Daddy went to bed. In the morning he told the children all that had happened, and you can guess how excited they were.

'Fancy our snowman saving us from robbers,' cried John. 'Oh, Jane, let's go and say thank you to him!'

So out they went, but, you know, it was a warm morning and the sun had been out for some time, so there was nothing much left of the snowman except a little heap of snow, Daddy's hat and gloves, and Mummy's scarf.

'Well, you were a fine snowman while you lasted!' said John. 'Thanks so much for all you did!'

The snowman didn't answer a word, but I expect he was pleased, all the same.

15

The Lost Slippers

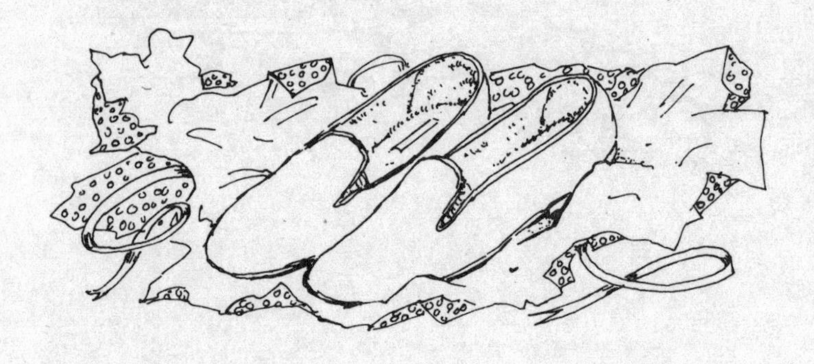

Daddy was very pleased because Mummy had given him a beautiful new pair of slippers for his birthday. They were bedroom slippers, very soft to wear, and lined inside with brown wool.

'Aha!' said Daddy, putting them on. 'Now my feet will be warm!'

Peter and Betty wished they had slippers like Daddy too.

'Mummy, our slippers are wearing out,' Betty said. 'Couldn't we have some small ones like Daddy's big ones? We would so love to be like Daddy!'

'Very well,' said Mummy. 'I will buy you some next week when we go by the shoe-shop.'

So very soon not only Daddy had nice warm bedroom slippers, but the two children had as well. They put them on and danced round the nursery in them.

'Look!' Betty cried to Cinders, the black cat. 'See my new slippers!'

'Look!' Peter called to Spot, the little terrier puppy. 'Don't you wish you had slippers like mine, Spot!'

Every night Daddy put his slippers on when he got home, and every night the two children put theirs on when they went upstairs to bed. Betty's were blue with brown wool inside, Peter's were yellow, and Daddy's were brown.

And then a strange thing happened.

The slippers began to disappear! First, one of Betty's went. Mummy was cross about it.

'Haven't I told you, Betty, to put your slippers away carefully when you get into bed?' said Mummy.

'But I *did,* Mummy!' cried Betty.

'Well, you couldn't have,' said Mummy. 'Or they would both be under your chair this morning.'

That night one of Daddy's slippers disappeared. It was really most mysterious. Nobody could understand it! Betty had put both Daddy's slippers to get warm by the fire - and when Daddy came in and sat down in his chair to take off his shoes - there was only one slipper for him to put on!

'Hey, Betty!' he called. 'Where's my other slipper, darling?'

'Isn't it by the fire, Daddy?' said Betty in astonishment. 'I put it there.'

'Have you been having a joke and hidden it, Peter?' asked Daddy. Peter was fond of playing tricks, and Daddy thought it might be Peter who had run

off with the slipper for fun. But Peter shook his head.

'No, Daddy, I haven't touched your slippers, really I haven't.'

'Well, it must be about the room somewhere, that lost slipper!' said Daddy. 'Hunt about and find it. Perhaps it is under my chair.'

The two children hunted about everywhere, but they could *not* find Daddy's slipper. So he had to put on his old ones, and he was quite cross about it.

The next slipper to disappear was one of Peter's! Yes, it really did. Peter knew quite well he had put them carefully under his chair when he got into bed - but the next night one was gone! Only one slipper stood under his chair.

'I say! This is getting a bit *too* mysterious,' said Peter. 'Is it magic, do you think, Betty?'

'I don't know,' said Betty, puzzled. 'It's so queer, Peter, because anyone who wanted the slippers to wear would take *both* - not one! All our slippers are different sizes - one is no use to anyone!'

Mummy was annoyed about the slippers.

'They *must* be somewhere!' she said. 'Betty and Peter, you must just hunt about everywhere today till you find them. It must be carelessness. There is no other explanation!'

'Come on, Cinders; come on, Spot, and help us to hunt for the slippers!' said Peter. So the cat and the dog and the two children hunted everywhere for the lost slippers.

They looked under all the beds. They lifted all the chairs. They hunted in

every cupboard. They even looked in the larder, though Cook said if they found any slippers there she would be *most* surprised. They didn't, of course.

Then they went to look behind the cushions. No, no slippers were there, either. It was most puzzling.

Cinders and Spot trotted all over the

place with the children, sniffing here and there. At last the children came to the shelf on which stood the three remaining slippers - one of Daddy's, one of Betty's, and one of Peter's. They did look funny, all odd, by themselves.

Spot ran up to one of the slippers, and took it into his mouth. He threw it up into the air, caught it, and then began to shake it like a rat. Then he ran off to his big, cosy basket with it.

'Hi, Spot, don't *you* steal any of our slippers!' cried Peter, and he ran after the puppy.

But Spot quickly tucked the slipper under his warm rug, and lay down on it, all his legs in the air!

'Betty! Perhaps *Spot* has taken our slippers!' cried Peter. He ran to the basket, and tipped the puppy out. Then he lifted up the big, warm rug - and what do you suppose he saw? Yes - you are quite right! All the lost slippers were there, as well as the one that Spot had just taken! There they were, neatly tucked under the rug, all a bit chewed.

'Mummy! Mummy! We've found the lost slippers!' cried Peter. 'Come and look!'

So Mummy came and when she saw where they were, how they laughed - and how they scolded the naughty puppy!

'We must keep them where he can't get them!' said Mummy. So now all the new slippers are kept safely in a cupboard, and Spot isn't allowed to put so much as a whisker inside the door.

'Now we can all have warm feet at night again!' cried Betty. 'You naughty little Spot! Wait till *you* have nice new slippers given you! I'll run off with *yours!*'

'Wuff!' said Spot. 'If you wait till *I* wear slippers, you'll wait a long time!'

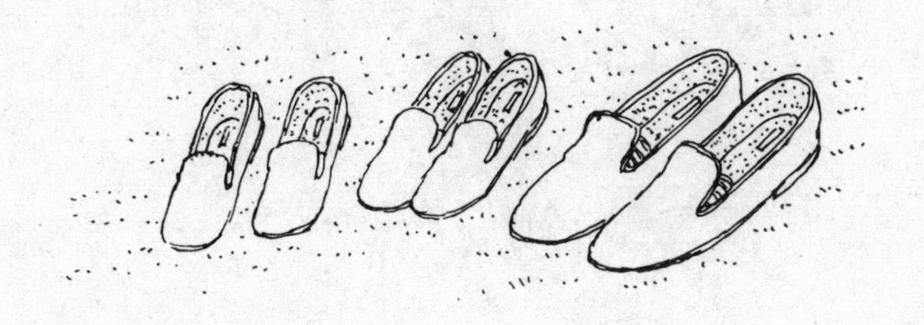

16

The Squirrel and the Pixie

There was once a pixie called Goldie because of her shining yellow hair. All the summer she played with the swallows in the air, and when they flew away in October she was sad.

'The cold days are coming,' twittered the swallows to her. 'We must go. You cannot come with us, Goldie, because your wings could not fly so far. Why do you not sleep through the cold days as many of the other creatures do?'

'I think I will,' said Goldie. So she set about making herself some warm rugs and blankets, a warm dress and a warm cloak.

'Then I shall be able to sleep in comfort,' she told a spider who was watching her. 'I shall roll myself up in all these warm clothes and sleep until the spring, just as you do, Spider.'

She made her blankets of rose-petals, sewn neatly together. She made her rugs of the thistledown that she gathered from the thistles - it looked like a furry cover when she had finished it. She sewed herself a dress and a coat of crimson creeper leaves, and she did look nice in them.

Then she went to find a place to sleep in. She chose a nice cosy corner at the bottom of some big Michaelmas daisies.

They waved their pretty daisy-heads far above her. She smiled at them.

'You will shelter me when it rains,' she said. Then she curled herself up in her new rugs and went to sleep.

But alas for poor Goldie! In a few days' time, the gardener came along and cut down all the Michaelmas

daisies! They were fading, and he wanted to make the garden tidy.

He very nearly trod on Goldie. She woke up in a great fright and flew away, leaving behind her beautiful warm rugs and blankets. She saw them all put into the gardener's barrow and wheeled away to be burnt on the bonfire. She was very unhappy.

'I am so cold,' she shivered. 'I shall not be able to make any more covers. I shall freeze to death at night!'

A small red squirrel bounded over to her. 'Why are you crying?' he asked. Goldie told him.

'Well, why don't you go and cuddle up to one of the little animals who sleep the winter days away?' he asked her. 'They usually have plenty of moss and dead leaves for blankets, or at any rate some sort of shelter from winter storms.'

'That's a very good idea,' said Goldie, cheering up. 'But where shall I find anybody? I don't know where to look.'

'Oh, I'll soon show you one or two,' said the squirrel. 'First of all, come and see the nice cosy hole that the hedgehog is sleeping in. He always makes himself very comfortable for the winter.'

Goldie took the squirrel's paw and he led her to a little hole in a dry bank. He pushed aside a mossy curtain and Goldie slipped inside. She saw a big, brown prickly hedgehog there, fast asleep, curled up warmly on some dead leaves.

She came out of the hole again and shook her head. 'No, dear Squirrel,' she said, 'I don't want to sleep with the hedgehog. He is so prickly that I couldn't cuddle up to him – and besides, he snores! Take me somewhere else.'

'Well, I'll take you to the toad,' said the squirrel. 'He always chooses a good, sheltered place.'

So he took the pixie to a big mossy stone, and told her to creep underneath it. There she found the old toad sleeping soundly, quite safe and cosy under the stone. But Goldie crept out again, shivering.

'He has no blankets to cover himself,' she said. 'And it is damp under there. I wouldn't like to sleep there.'

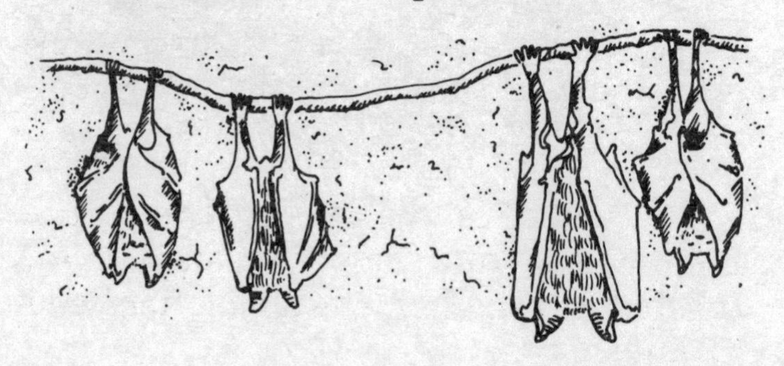

'Well, come where the bats live,' said the squirrel. 'They sleep very soundly indeed.' So he took her to an old cave and showed her the black bats hanging upside down around the cave. But Goldie screwed up her little nose and ran outside the cave.

'They smell,' she said. 'I couldn't possibly sleep with the bats.'

The squirrel thought for a moment. 'You might like to cuddle in a heap with the snakes,' he said. 'They have chosen a good hollow tree this winter, and they are so comfortable there. Come along. I'll show you.'

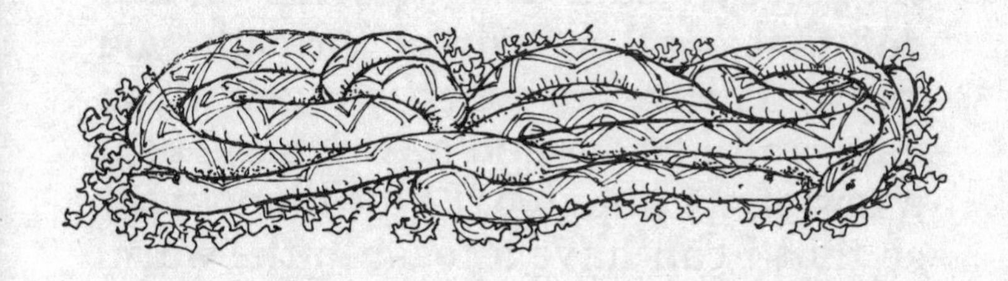

But when Goldie peeped inside the hollow tree and saw the snakes all twisted up together, she shook her head at once.

'No,' she said. 'I wouldn't dare to sleep with the snakes! See how they have twisted themselves together, Squirrel! They might squeeze me to bits if they twisted round me too! No! Show me someone else, please.'

'You are very hard to please, Goldie,' said the squirrel, thinking hard. 'There's the dormouse - he has quite a nice winter nest in the roots of the old fir tree. Would you like to go there?'

'Oh, I don't think so,' said Goldie. 'It sounds too stuffy to me. What about *you*, Squirrel? Where do *you* sleep?'

'Oh, I sleep in a hole in a tree, and am very cosy,' said the squirrel. 'But I don't sleep all the winter through, you know. I wake up when we get warm days and I go out and have a play. I eat a few of my nuts too. I hide them away so that I can have a feast in the warm winter days - we do get quite nice sunny days sometimes, you know, and I always think it's such a pity to sleep through those.'

'I agree with you!' cried Goldie

joyfully. 'I'd like to wake up sometimes too, and have a feast of nuts.'

'The only thing is – I often forget where I hide my nuts,' said the squirrel. 'I'd love to have you share my sleeping-hole, Goldie, if you'd help me to hunt for my nuts when we wake.'

'I'll help you, I'll help you!' cried Goldie. 'Now, show me where you sleep, Squirrel.'

So he showed her his warm, sheltered hole in the oak tree, and together they curled up there, warm and happy. Goldie cuddled right into the squirrel's lovely fur, and it was just like a cosy rug.

'I'm so happy,' she said sleepily. 'This is better than squeezing in with the snakes – or getting a cold under the toad's stone – or hanging upside down with the bats! Good night, dear Squirrel! Sleep tight!'

They did – and on the first warm winter days they will wake, and you may see them hunting for the nuts that the squirrel so carefully hid away in

October. If you see him, look out for Goldie - she is very much better at finding the nuts than he is!

17

Ha, Ha, Jack-in-the-Box!

Of all the toys in the nursery the greatest nuisance was the Jack-in-the-box! He was for ever jumping out of his box just when nobody was expecting him, and this was most upsetting, especially to timid creatures like the pink rabbit and the baby doll.

But the Jack-in-the-box simply loved to scare people. He thought it was great fun. He was an ugly creature, with a big red face, two little arms, and a big pink body made of a long spring. When his lid sprang open and he jumped out, he shook and jerked on his spring in a most peculiar manner. Nobody liked him.

Ha, Ha, Jack-in-the-Box!

His box was shut by a little catch. By slipping out his arm the Jack-in-the-box could undo his catch whenever he wanted to - then his lid would fly up and he would spring out to his full length, jerking and bouncing about in a most terrifying manner! It was a pity he could undo his own box.

One day he waited in a dark corner for the baby doll to come by, and when she trotted past, click! went his lid, and out he jumped with a yell. The baby doll fell down in fright and turned blue in the face. This made her look very strange, and it took the toys all night to get her face the right colour again. The Jack-in-the-box looked on and made rude remarks all the time.

'One day you'll go too far,' said the teddy bear angrily. 'Why don't you frighten people your own size? Me, for instance!'

'All right!' said the Jack-in-the-box. 'I'll give you a real scare, teddy!'

'Pooh, *I'm* not afraid of you!' said the teddy, and he gave the Jack-in-the-box a smack on his red, grinning face. The Jack-in-the-box was angry and jumped after the teddy bear all over the nursery floor, making a great noise each time his box came down bang on the floor.

After that he lay in wait for the bear. He saw one night that Mollie, the little

girl to whom all the toys belonged, had left a bowl of soapy water on the floor. She had been blowing big bubbles. The Jack-in-the-box placed himself just nearby and waited for the bear to come by. Soon, along he came, whistling a little tune.

'Bo!' The Jack-in-the-box sprang right out of his box, and gave the bear such a terrible scare that he fell right into the bowl of soapy water - which was just what the Jack-in-the-box meant him to do.

The Jack-in-the-box laughed so much at the sight of the bear swimming about in the water, that big tears ran all down his pink body.

'You horrid creature!' said the bear, climbing out. 'I hope your tears rust your springs!'

He had to stand by the fire all night long to dry himself - and even when morning came he was a bit damp. So he got a dreadful cold and sneezed twenty times without stopping, which was very tiring.

The next night the Jack-in-the-box jumped out at the pink rabbit and frightened him so much that he tried to get down a crack in the floor boards and stuck half-way. It was very difficult to get him out, but the toys managed to at last.

'We won't have anything to do with that horrid Jack-in-the-box,' said the toys to one another. 'We won't speak to him. We won't answer him. We won't look at him. We won't ask him to any parties!'

'And we'll have a perfectly wonderful party very very soon!' said the rag doll. 'Then when the Jack-in-the-box sees that he isn't even asked, he will be sorry for his bad ways!'

So a wonderful party was arranged for Friday night. There were to be chocolate buns and toffee to eat, cooked on the toy stove by the pink rabbit, who was a very good cook indeed. There was to be lemonade drunk out of the cups belonging to the doll's teaset. There were to be games of all kinds and dancing to the music of the musical box. The rag doll said they could all take turns at turning the handle round.

Everyone was asked except the Jack-in-the-box. He was furious.

'What! You're not going to ask *me!*' he cried in a rage. 'Very well, then – I'll come to your party *without* being asked – and I'll jump all over the place and upset the lemonade and squash the chocolate buns – so there! Not ask me, indeed! Whatever next!'

The toys stared at one another in dismay. They hadn't thought of that. Now what were they to do?

The teddy bear beckoned to the rag doll. They went into a corner and whispered.

'I've a plan,' said the bear. 'If only I'm brave enough to carry it out!'

'What is it?' asked the rag doll.

'Well, what about nailing down the Jack-in-the-box's lid?' asked the bear. 'I know where the hammer and nails are kept – in Mollie's little carpentry set. When he is asleep I could take a nail, creep up to his box and nail down his lid!'

'That's a splendid idea – if only you are brave enough!' said the rag doll.

The teddy bear didn't feel brave enough until early on Friday night, an hour before the party was to begin. The rag doll told him that the Jack-in-the-box was asleep, because she had heard him snoring. The bear ran to the toolbox and took out a hammer and a big nail.Then he crept bravely up to the Jack-in-the-box. Bang, bang! He drove the nail through the lid into the edge of the box!

The Jack-in-the-box woke up. He slipped out his arm and undid his catch - but what was this! His lid did not spring open as it usually did! He could not get out! He began to jerk about in his box in a rage, and the box jiggled and jolted.

'Now let the party begin!' cried the big doll. 'The rabbit has made the buns and the toffee and I have poured out the lemonade in the cups!'

'Let me out, let me out!' shouted the Jack-in-the-box angrily. But nobody did. The party went on merrily. All the buns and the toffee were eaten, and there was no more lemonade left. The rag doll turned the handle of the musical box and the toys began to dance. What fun!

The Jack-in-the-box was taken no notice of at all. He tried his best to get out but the nail was much too strong. He had to stay shut in his box whilst the toys had a fine time.

The next day Mollie had a friend to tea, and the little boy picked up the Jack-in-the-box and tried to open the box.

'How funny, Mollie! It's nailed up!' he said. 'Why did you do that?'

'I didn't,' said Mollie, in surprise. 'Let me look.'

'Well,' she said, 'I don't know who nailed him up – but I think it's a good idea! I never did like him! He can stay nailed up!'

And for all I know the Jack-in-the-box is still tightly fastened in his box –

but I dare say if he gives his solemn promise to the rag doll to behave himself in future, the toys will forgive him and take out the nail.

It was a good punishment for him, wasn't it?